DEFENDERS
KILLING GROUND

TOM PALMER

With illustrations by
David Shephard

onkers

First published in 2017 in Great Britain by
Barrington Stoke Ltd
18 Walker Street, Edinburgh, EH3 7LP

www.barringtonstoke.co.uk

Reprinted 2018

Text © 2017 Tom Palmer
Illustrations © 2017 David Shephard

A CIP catalogue record for this book is available
from the British Library upon request

ISBN: 978-1-78112-729-2

Printed and bound in Great Britain by Clays Ltd, Elcograf S.p.A.

For Newcastle School for Boys.
Thank you for helping me to write Defenders.

The Vikings invaded Yorkshire in the year 866. They attacked an Anglo-Saxon village at night in a place that sounds just like where we live now.

They slaughtered men, women and children. They made this place into a terrible killing ground of blood and fire.

1

Seth could not forget the face he'd seen in the flames at the Shay Stadium.

Its tangle of long hair, its leathery skin streaked with black. The memory filled Seth with a dread that he was convinced would never leave him.

His heart raced every time the dark and fiery face came back to him.

It was a feeling far worse than when his football team were hammered five nil at home.

Worse than when he broke his leg when he was a kid. Even worse than the day his mum had sat him down and told him she was seriously ill.

Seth didn't understand how he could possibly feel worse than that.

But he did when he remembered the face, the flames and the stench of death that scorched his nostrils.

Seth knew that strange forces were at work in the stadium.

But why?

And who did the face belong to?

Seth had no choice but to find out.

2

It had all started when the new floodlights came on at half-time. That's when it all started.

Seth and his mum were in their usual seats at FC Halifax Town's Shay Stadium. Halifax were two up, both goals coming from Seth's favourite player, Ian Oldfield. The club groundsman, Ernie, came to lean on the low wall in front of Seth's front row seat to the right of the substitutes' bench.

Seth knew Ernie from his school work

experience at the club last term. He liked his mischievous grin and how the wrinkles around his pale eyes bunched together as if he'd been smiling all his life.

"What do you think, Seth? About the new lights?"

"I think they're brilliant," Seth said, and Ernie beamed nearly as bright as the lights themselves.

For the seventy years that The Shay had been FC Halifax Town's stadium, there had been four floodlight stanchions, one at each corner of the pitch. Now it had a circle of thirty individual lights attached to the tops of the stands.

"Good lad." Ernie winked, then turned to Seth's mum. "And how are you doing, Mrs White?"

Seth continued to gaze at the lights on top of the stand opposite as the two adults spoke. Ernie wasn't just being polite with his question. He was

asking about Seth's mum's health. Cancer was a word Seth didn't like to say out loud. But he could think it. It echoed around his head, as relentless as a car alarm left on all night.

"I start my treatment soon," Seth's mum told Ernie. "With a specialist down in London. After that, I'll be better in no time."

Seth stared even harder at the lights, deliberately making his eyes hurt. In truth, he didn't like the new floodlights. He preferred how they used to be – when he was younger and his mum wasn't ill. But the lights had changed and so had his life. There was no going back.

Seth blanked out the conversation between his mum and Ernie, and instead imagined Halifax Town supporters of seventy years ago, watching matches in the cold. He could almost see them in their long coats and thick woollen football scarves.

Ernie put his hand on Seth's shoulder. "Two nil up," he said. "New floodlights in good working order. It's all going to plan, Seth."

"It is," Seth replied, trying to smile.

He wouldn't forget saying those words because things were about to stop going to plan. They were about to start going seriously wrong.

3

As soon as the second half kicked off the weather changed, a sudden summer storm flashing overhead, bringing thunder and rolling dark clouds and rain.

The ball was more under the control of the wind than the players.

Seth watched one of the Halifax defenders clear a corner, only to see the ball swirl back on itself, into the path of a Wrexham striker who controlled it and fired it at goal.

2–1.

Now the opposition were pushing for an equaliser.

Unable to watch, Seth stared at the trees thrashing around behind the South Stand. What was going on? The weather had been beautiful all day. He listened to the fans' chant of *Shaymen! Shaymen!* echo through the stands.

But the chanting wasn't enough to stop Halifax Town conceding again five minutes later. More chaos caused by the wind.

2–2.

Seth's mum said nothing. She stared down at the pitch and so did Seth, like they always did when their team let in a goal. It was one of their unspoken rules.

But it was hard to focus on the pitch tonight. The wind rattling around the ground was so loud it sounded like the stadium roof was about to fly

off into the night. The storm was dashing the trees against the back of the South Stand, playing the corrugated iron like a drum. Hail fell in a curtain across the pitch, dimming the brightness of the new lights. Seth could smell electrical burning. And something else. Something rotten or sour.

He looked up to see the floodlights going out one by one, replaced by a strange glow swirling around the pitch.

Like flames.

This was no ordinary storm.

Then Seth heard an ear-splitting crack.

Like everyone else in the crowd, Seth looked instantly to his left. The giant oak, which had stood at the far end of the Shay for over a hundred years, was shaking.

Something was about to happen. Everyone knew it. Even the players were staring.

Then a second crack. Even louder this time, as one of the big branches of the great oak tree sheared off with a roar, crushing the corner of the Skircoat Stand, with a creak of tearing metal and splintering wood.

Screams.

Shouts.

People running for cover.

All drowned out by the howling wind.

Seth knew he had to get his mum out of there. And fast.

4

Seth grabbed his mum's arm. "Let's go," he said, just as an announcement came over the tannoy.

"Ladies and gentlemen," a calm voice said. "The game has been abandoned. The stadium is unsafe. Please leave immediately by walking onto the pitch and then through the North Stand, where stewards will assist you."

Seth took his mum's hand and led her onto the

pitch. She had been quiet since her conversation with Ernie and Seth knew she was tired.

Seth felt bad. Not because of the storm raging around him. Not because he wished his mum was safe at home when she was so ill. There was something else. A deep-down feeling inside his chest.

Dread.

Dread that something much, much worse was going to happen.

"Come on, Mum," Seth said, breathless from the intensity of feeling in his chest.

His mum followed silently as wind roared across the pitch. They joined hundreds of fans staggering across the grass towards the corner of the North Stand. Seth looked behind him one last time before they left the pitch. The trees around the edge of the stadium seemed to be on fire. Or were his eyes playing tricks on him?

That light like flames again.

What was that?

And why was he seeing it?

Then – amid the flames – Seth saw a face. The wild face of a man with black marks streaked down his cheeks, framed by long flowing hair.

A Viking. That was Seth's first thought.

The man looked like pictures of Vikings he'd seen in books at school. He'd enjoyed learning about the violent events in Britain over 1,000 years ago.

But this was no history project. This man was real, present.

Seth turned away and pushed on under the stand with his mum. The spinning of the turnstiles made a horrendous clattering noise. Then they were out of the stadium. Onto the street. And, echoing off the hills around Halifax, was the sound of sirens heading to the Shay.

"Did you see the flames?" Seth asked his mum.

Mum shook her head, her face pale. Seth had to get her home.

And luckily home was just a three-minute walk away.

5

Seth and his mum walked slowly up the hill of terraced houses. When Seth opened their front door, a large dog lunged at him.

"Rosa," Seth shouted. "Down."

Rosa – black and wiry – stopped barking and dropped a mangled grey womble at Seth's feet, withdrew a few steps, then stared at him, her back legs trembling like coiled springs.

Seth lunged at Rosa and rolled her onto the

floor, so his mum could come in from the rain and slump onto the sofa in the front room. His mum was shattered and she needed looking after. That was Seth's job. And part of the job was to keep Rosa away from her.

Seth kicked the womble down the hall, then shouted, "Stay."

Rosa sat with the toy between her paws, then rested her chin on the varnished wooden floor.

His mum was clearly exhausted, but Seth was surprised she had made it to the football that night at all. She'd had a minor operation that morning. Something to do with the treatment she was going to have at the hospital in London. Seth had said that they could miss the game, but she'd been determined to go.

"We've not missed one for years," she'd said. "And my being ill isn't going to stop that. This cancer isn't going to stop anything."

But now his mum was paying for her bravery.

"Do you want your tablets?" Seth asked.

"Yes please."

"And a cup of tea?"

"Thanks, Seth. You're a star," his mum told him. "Can you take the washing out of the machine and hang it up? Please."

"Sure," Seth said.

Then he got on with it. He did what needed doing. He looked after his mum. Tea. Tablets. Laundry. Washing up.

Rosa followed him around the house, occasionally dropping the womble at his feet.

"Later," Seth told her. "I have stuff to do first. Sorry, Rosa."

It was ten-thirty when Seth helped his mum to bed. He turned the light off and quietly pulled the door to. Doing for her what she – and she alone –

had done for him for the first eleven years of his life.

Seth had never had a dad. His dad had died before he was born. It was a fact. It was normal. It was fine.

But now, with his mum being so ill, and after the weirdest of nights, Seth missed the presence of a dad more than ever.

6

Outside, the wind had died down and the clouds were dispersing to reveal a clear black sky. With the Shay floodlights off, Seth could see silvery shadows cast by the moon.

Seth walked Rosa over Huddersfield Road and towards the stadium. The Shay was surrounded by steep banks covered with trees and bushes, places Rosa liked to snuffle and scamper in. Her favourite patch was a triangle of woods on the corner of the

ground, opposite the bus depot. Seth released Rosa into the woods. She tore into the bushes, slaloming trees, barking and whimpering.

Seth knew it would take ages to get his dog out of her little wood. But she loved it so much, he always let her off the lead there. She'd been patient all night waiting for him. Now it was her time.

Seth stared into the Shay – it was empty. Ernie would be long gone. He'd perhaps be having a pint in the pub over the road.

So, what were the noises Seth could hear coming from the stadium?

Noises like shouts. Or laughter.

Seth guessed it was probably drinkers passing on their way back from town, not people in the stadium at all. It was nearly eleven and the pubs would be starting to empty.

Then Rosa was next to him, leaning heavily

against his leg. Staring at him with big brown eyes, reflecting street-light orange. And Seth could smell something in the undergrowth. Something musty.

"What's up, Rosa?" Seth was surprised that she'd had enough already.

Rosa whined the whine she whined on bonfire night when she hid under the kitchen table. Afraid she might bolt, Seth slipped her lead on, then peered again into the Shay through the woods at the gap between the two corner stands.

Seth saw flickering like torchlight shining in the stadium. There *was* something happening on the pitch. There were patterns of light and shadow. Or flames, like before. But it was so hard to tell what it was or where it was coming from.

And now Rosa was pulling hard at her lead, her nose pointing towards home.

Seth went with her, craning his neck

backwards. His whole body was alert with tension, the hairs on his arms on end, his head thumping. And he felt that dread again. The dark, heavy feeling that he didn't understand, but that told him something bad was coming.

"Come on," he said to Rosa, as he felt a shiver go down the back of his neck right the way down to his toes.

*

Back home, Rosa followed Seth into his room. She slumped at the foot of his bed and gave a very human sigh.

Seth patted her on the head, then grabbed a comic off his stack, climbed into bed and started to read.

Another day – another superhero comic.

Seth had over 2,000 comics. They were his dad's complete collection. All Seth's now.

Seth loved them. Really loved them. From the first time he'd picked one up, before he'd even started school, he'd imagined that the superhero – whichever one it was – was his dad. That's where his dad was for him now. Between the pages of these comics. For Seth, it was how he spent time with him.

The comics made Seth feel good. He wanted everything to be calm, to be normal. But today, as Seth read, a dark sense of trouble to come was simmering below the surface.

7

That Wednesday afternoon after Maths, Seth half
ran down the main corridor of Manor Heath School.
If he was quick he'd avoid the rush before the other
classes filled the corridor and blocked the staircases.

He knew it might seem odd, but Seth loved
these old, tiled corridors. When they were empty,
it was easy to imagine all the children who'd ever
been to this school walking along them in their old-
fashioned uniforms. Seth felt like he could actually

see them, his imagining of them was so vivid.

Seth had told his mum about it once. About how he sometimes felt like he could see people from the past, at school or on the streets around where they lived, but she'd gone all weird with him. In the same way she'd go weird when he asked about his dad. Seth loved his mum, so when she was funny about things like that, he'd leave her be and try to forget whatever he'd wanted to ask.

"Seth," a voice called. "*Seth!*"

Seth carried on walking. He needed time on his own. All day, he'd been trying to piece together all that had happened last night at the Shay. The lights. The storm. The gloom he'd been feeling. That face with its frame of wild hair.

"Seth – *stop!*"

Now there were footsteps. Someone was running after him.

Seth turned round. It was Nadiya. They'd gone to the same junior school together, although they'd barely talked since starting at Manor Heath, mainly because they were in different forms.

"Seth. Wait. I wanted to ask you ..." Nadiya stopped running. She took a long breath and smiled. "To ask you if you're OK. Today you've looked ... so sad."

Seth was surprised that what he'd been feeling inside had shown on his face. And that someone might have noticed. But, if anyone was going to notice, it would be Nadiya. Nadiya was clever. Really clever. She was a pupil librarian at the school because she loved books so much. Seth knew that she loved history too. She was fascinated – almost obsessed – with how things were in the past.

But Nadiya was more than book clever. She was sharp – at junior school she'd always been able to

think things through, work them out. Forever asking questions, questions that showed she looked at the world in ways that surprised even the teachers.

Seth had a thought. Perhaps Nadiya could help him. He couldn't talk to his mum about last night, not while she was ill. So Seth decided to tell Nadiya everything.

The storm.

The falling tree.

The noises.

The wild Viking face.

The strange swirling circle of fire.

Nadiya asked questions as they walked out of school, out onto the moor, the huge grass fields surrounded by posh houses at the top of Halifax.

As they walked across the moor, Seth could see a cluster of tents, no more than shadows, with smoke twisting out of them – he felt like he could

smell the fire smoke. He saw a handful of people there, too.

But Seth made himself ignore all that. He'd just told Nadiya about last night. Now he would find out if she believed him.

8

"Can you show me?" Nadiya asked. "Next time?" Her voice was serious, gentle, not mocking.

"Really?"

"Yeah," she said. "I'm interested in stuff like that."

They were nearly across the moor when Seth saw a man standing outside one of the big houses, watching them as they approached from the school. He was wearing a suit, a bunch of keys in his hand.

"There's my dad," Nadiya said, as they passed

over a rough circle of burned grass. "He's not got used to me walking across the moor on my own yet. He still wishes I was in junior school."

A sharp memory came back to Seth – of Nadiya's dad in his suit at their school gates with the other parents. Seth used to envy Nadiya for that, he was jealous of anyone whose dad was there at the gates for them.

And there he was now, in front of their house.

"Does your dad still work at the hospital?" Seth asked.

"Yeah."

When they reached Nadiya's dad he said, "Hello, Seth," then put his hand on Seth's shoulder. "How's your mother doing?"

Seth flinched at the question. He preferred to think about his mum on his own terms, and when he was alone and safe. Not to talk about her.

"OK, thanks," Seth spluttered. "She's going to London soon. To a special hospital."

"And she's not too tired?"

Seth found he couldn't speak now and so he shook his head.

Nadiya's dad recognised Seth was struggling. "If you need to talk, let me know."

"Err, yes – thanks," Seth said.

He waved goodbye, then went over the crossing, past St Jude's church, and down School Lane towards his house and the Shay at the bottom. All the time, he was aware of people walking with him or coming the other way. Real people and the people in his head.

Seth saw the shadows of mill-workers trudging home. A woman with an old-fashioned pram. A pair of soldiers, rifles slung across their backs. Seth often imagined what his town must have been like

in the past. He'd always done it – and his imaginings had always taken on these shadowy forms. He saw people as they were in history. He'd seen them moving up and down this road.

But there was something new today. The huts he'd seen on the moor. The whiff of smoke rising into the air. What had that been? He'd never experienced it before. Why was he seeing and smelling new things just now?

Seth opened the gate to his garden, clicked it shut behind him and leaned against it. He sighed. He was OK here. Safe.

Except Seth knew that, the closer he got to the Shay, the more uneasy he felt. And that presented a problem. In three days' time Halifax Town had their next home game – and Seth hadn't missed a home game for eight years.

9

Catastrophe.

By half-time, it was three–nil to Stockport. Seth's mum put her hand on his arm.

"You can have another bag of Haribos if you want," she said with a grin.

Seth laughed. He always had a bag of Haribos on match days. It had started when he was a kid and, deep down, he still liked it. He'd have them at kick-off or half-time. But he was only allowed one

bag and he'd already had today's at kick-off.

"OK, but I'll get it, Mum." Seth couldn't help but look at his mum in her woolly hat. Worn not because she was cold, but because the cancer treatment made her hair fall out.

"No, I'll go. I'm better today." His mum narrowed her eyes. "Don't do everything for me, Seth," she said in a quiet voice.

Seth gave way – she didn't need an argument about a bag of sweets.

As his mum walked along the row, Seth noticed people giving him sympathetic looks. He even felt a supportive hand on his back. People knew his mum was ill and they were being nice. That was clear. But Seth came to the Shay for football, not sympathy.

He swallowed and stared at the pitch. Ernie was out there, replacing chunks of turf that the players had ripped up with their studs. The pitch

was a mess. Heavy rain had poured down for the whole game. Seth wished he could go out and help Ernie. Sorting the turf was one job they'd done when he was here on his school work experience. That day had been the best.

"Here you go," Seth's mum said, returning with his Haribos. "Don't say I don't spoil you ..."

"Thanks, Mum."

The second half kicked off and as the match went on, Halifax conceded another goal. The final score was 0–4. Once the final whistle blew, people stood, preparing to venture out into the relentless rain.

Seth saw Ernie come onto the pitch jabbing at it with his fork even before the players had jogged off. Then he and his mum walked out of the back of the stadium. Up the slope. Across the road. Nipping into the shop to buy something for tea.

When they came out of the shop, Seth noticed that the Shay's floodlights had come on. Ernie must need the light – he'd be in for a long evening. Seth noticed, too, that the weather was getting worse. The wind was suddenly stronger, the clouds darker. Another storm was on its way.

10

Hours later, when Seth was brushing his teeth, he saw that the Shay floodlights were still on.

It's a long time to be replacing ripped up divots of grass, he thought. But Seth knew that Ernie was a perfectionist, that he would fix his pitch in high winds and driving rain if he needed to. Even if lightning was flashing across the sky.

Seth shrugged and went to bed to read his copy of *FourFourTwo*. At ten o'clock he switched

off his lamp. Light from the stadium floodlights cast shadowy outlines of trees and telephone wires through his blind and into his bedroom.

The storm was still going strong. After every boom of thunder Seth heard a low growl from Rosa.

"It's OK, Rosa," he said.

And every time he said it he heard Rosa's tail thump against the floor three times.

Seth closed his eyes and tried to sleep. But, in the dark, flames flickered like the ones he'd seen when the match was abandoned the week before. He tried to ignore them, but they wouldn't go away. So instead he looked at the flames more closely.

And, when he did, he saw the Viking face.

The man.

The beard.

The black markings across his eyes, as he stared into the storm.

Seth could smell a musty meaty reek too.

He sensed that the man was not just looking wildly into the wind and rain, but that he was staring at him, Seth. Into Seth's eyes. Into Seth's mind.

Seth snapped his eyes open.

What was that about? He shuddered and looked at his clock. It said 04:01.

Four o'clock? Really? He'd only just switched his light off.

Seth looked up at his skylight window. It was dark outside. Dark, but not dark. The Shay floodlights still lit up the night sky.

Now Seth knew that something really was wrong.

11

Seth sat up and saw a pair of dark eyes at the foot of his bed.

Rosa, watching him.

"What?" Seth asked.

Rosa stood up, walked to the door and eyed him over her shoulder. She'd left her womble on the floor next to her blanket.

Seth sighed. Rosa wanted to go out.

He got out of bed and walked along the landing

and down the stairs. Rosa followed. It amazed him how soundlessly she could walk on the varnished floorboards at night. She always made a proper racket with her nails in the daytime.

Seth put on his coat, then opened the front door, allowing Rosa to push past him to do what she needed to do. He sat on the step and waited, enjoying the fresh outside air, staring up at the trees as the wind tossed them about. And, now that he was fully awake, he had a question.

"Why are the floodlights still on?" he asked Rosa.

But Rosa just looked at him with her gentle eyes.

"Come on," Seth said, attaching the lead to Rosa's collar and taking her down the garden path.

But Rosa wasn't keen. She was pulling to go back into the house.

Seth had to drag her out of the gate and down the hill, past the night-shuttered shops and over the Huddersfield Road. He could see mill-workers making their way down the street in dribs and drabs, the sky starting to brighten behind Beacon Hill to the east.

The hour before dawn. It was cold and the wind was still wild. Rosa's woods were noisy with rustling and clicks, but she was pulling harder now, trying to bring the walk to an end.

But Seth was determined. The new floodlights were still on, shining bright.

Why?

He took out his phone and scanned social media, thinking that West Yorkshire Police or FC Halifax Town might have tweeted to explain what was going on.

There was nothing.

Seth approached the Shay with care. He knew

he could see over a fence and into the stadium over the Skircoat Stand, through Rosa's woods. He'd have a look from there, then call the police, if there was anything to report.

Seth stood on tiptoe at the fence. All he could see was the pitch illuminated. No divots now. Ernie had done a good job. Seth was trying to make sense of what looked like tyre or burn marks across the pitch when he heard a vehicle and saw a new source of light. Flashing blue light.

He dragged Rosa round the back of the stadium and down towards the far end of the car park. There he saw an ambulance, a police car and a group in dark uniforms. Then Seth saw flames in the trees all around and above him.

Now Rosa was pulling hard for home. Seth went with her, not resisting. She was right to be afraid. He was too.

44

Seth didn't look back, worried he'd see more than just flames. The flames were weird, but they were just flames. More than anything, Seth didn't want to see that Viking face with its beard and dark markings. He never wanted to see it again. Or smell the stench of rotting meat that came with it.

As Rosa dragged him home, the floodlights flickered off and the wind dropped. Seth rushed into the house to see what he could find online about what had happened at the Shay.

There was nothing.

But what he needed to know came two hours later.

12

Nadiya's text arrived at 6.30 a.m.

I've got something to tell you. About the
Shay. N

Seth walked up School Lane to Nadiya's house.
As soon as he reached the edge of the moor, he
saw smoke rising from the tents he'd seen the day
before. But now he could see that they weren't tents.

They were wooden huts.

Some had thatched roofs. There were fences made of thin branches woven together. It was like something from over one thousand years ago. Certainly before there were proper buildings in Halifax. Before bricks and tiles and roads and pavements. As well as the smell of smoke, Seth could hear the *chink chink chink* of a hammer striking metal, see the light of a fire glowing, then fading.

Shadows.

He'd always seen shadows, but he'd never seen shadows quite like this. Before, it had always been people heading for work in the mills. Men in suits and hats, or in heavy coats and overalls. Women in long dresses and shawls. These shadows seemed different, as if they were from further back in history.

It had never occurred to Seth that hundreds of years ago people might have lived out on this moor. So, why was he seeing them – smelling and hearing them, too?

Seth decided he'd tell Nadiya what he'd seen last night. But not until she'd told him what her piece of news was. That was the priority.

Seth had no idea what she knew or how she knew it. He was here to find out. So, once again, he tried to forget about the shadows, so he could concentrate on what Nadiya had to say.

"What is it?" he asked, crossing the road towards her.

"My dad was at the hospital last night," Nadiya started. "Working in A&E."

Now Seth knew what this was about. "The ambulance?" he asked. "At the Shay?"

"Yes," Nadiya went on. "They found the

groundsman on the pitch in the early hours of the morning."

Ernie. Seth's chest tightened. He stared into Nadiya's eyes, still listening.

"He'd collapsed," she said. "And ..."

"Is he dead?" Seth gasped.

Nadiya shook her head. "No. He's in intensive care – in a coma, but alive."

"What happened?"

"Dad doesn't know. But the paramedics did tell him –"

"What?" Seth interrupted.

"That there were marks on the pitch where they found him."

"What?"

"Burned grass," Nadiya said. "Like there'd been a fire. And the scorch marks made a perfect circle."

13

At morning break Seth walked out of school and sat on the moor. The sun was blazing and the grass was dry, good to sit on. He was alone. And that was how he wanted to be.

Dozens of other children were standing or sitting in groups, talking. But Seth was oblivious to them. Oblivious, too, to the cluster of wooden huts ranged out across the grass. He was looking at his phone. Social media. News sites. Then he was

staring into space to try to work everything out.

Ernie. What had happened to him?

The *Halifax Courier* website had a short piece about the groundsman. It stated that he'd been found in the middle of the night, in mysterious circumstances. Police were studying CCTV. The *Courier* made no mention of the strange discovery on the pitch.

But social media had wind of the burned circle. Some said it was caused by a UFO landing. Others thought Ernie had disturbed a pagan ritual on the pitch. People from all over the world offered their opinions. Seth guessed that most of them had never been to Halifax.

And Seth was sure that their opinions were nonsense.

All of them.

He stood up and walked away from the school,

down the hill. He'd seen a circle like the one scorched onto the football pitch before. Here on the moor. Not so long ago.

The thought of the circle burned in Seth's mind and now he was running fast, voices and laughter from the school fading away.

14

Seth ran down the moor to where he thought he'd seen the circle of burned grass. He sprinted past the shadows of the wooden huts, more vivid than ever. He could smell smoke from their wood fires and the earthy whiff of animals clustered in pens near the dwellings.

Seth ran to where he'd walked with Nadiya the day before. The place where they'd looked up and first seen her dad. The place where he'd seen a circle of flames scorching the dry grass.

But now he wondered if he'd imagined it at all. Could it be that he'd actually seen it? Could it be that all the things he'd always thought were in his imagination were real? The shadows of workers walking to the mill. Old-fashioned children in the corridors at school.

And, if they were real, what did that mean?

Seth stopped.

He understood.

Those figures from his town's past that he'd always thought were imaginings were real.

Real, like the Anglo-Saxon village he was walking through now was real. Real like the woman sitting on her heels using a stick to stir a large clay pot, gold glittering at her neck. Real like the child playing next to her, spinning wooden disks with symbols on them. Real like the burned circle Seth was staring at right now.

Real like Ernie in a coma in intensive care. All of it real.

And the face of that man. Was that real too? Would he see it again? And, if it was real, what did it mean?

Then Seth thought about his mum. About why she acted odd about the things he saw. About why, when he asked about his dad, she wouldn't answer properly, or would look away, or change the subject. There was a link, Seth realised. But what was it? And how could he find out what joined all these things together?

Now Seth was running back up the moor, through clusters of school kids, two or three calling out to him. But he ignored them all, fixed on his purpose.

He needed to get to the library. To Nadiya. She was the only person who would understand and – perhaps – the only person who could help.

15

"I know what's going on," Seth said, his voice coming out too loud.

"What?" Nadiya was staring at him like he'd lost the plot.

"I know what it is."

"Seth. Calm down. You're not making sense. You know what *what* is?"

Seth took a few breaths, trying to steady himself. To calm his heartbeat. To settle the chaos

in his brain. He knew that other students in the library were watching him, but pretending not to. All of them hoping something dramatic was about to happen. Seth looked around at the large wooden desks, the shelves stacked with books and magazines. Tried to take in the calm.

He lowered his voice. "These things I'm seeing," he told Nadiya. "And hearing. The things I've always seen. They're not in my imagination. They're real. And the circle of fire at the Shay. There's one on the moor too."

"I know."

"And they're connected," Seth went on. "It's something to do with things that happened on the moor. Real events. In the past. Just like the mill-workers I see are real. And the children in the school corridors. I need to find out what and why and when. Because ..."

Seth stopped talking and stared at his friend. "What did you say?" he asked.

Nadiya was looking at Seth quizzically. "I know," she said. "And I want to help you."

16

Seth shivered as he and Nadiya walked across the moor together. It had been warm, but now the bright blue open sky was drawing off all the heat of the day.

"Describe what you told me about," Nadiya said. "Everything."

"The things I can see?"

Seth looked at the scene ahead of him. It was familiar to him now. Then he did his best to bring it to life for Nadiya. The cluster of wooden huts with

roofs thatched with straw or grass. Smoke rising out of the thatch. The fenced pens of sheep and goats. People in rough woven clothes going about their business. Looking after animals. Working metal over a fire. Grinding grain between two round stones.

When he finished, Nadiya was grinning. "That sounds so like what archaeologists think Anglo-Saxon settlements were like," she said. "The houses. The small farms. Do you remember learning about it at school?"

"Sort of," Seth said.

Nadiya was on a roll. "Then the Vikings came and attacked Anglo-Saxon villages. They burned them down. And stole anything they could, including young women. Could what you're seeing be connected with that? The wild Viking face? The settlement of Anglo-Saxon homes?"

"I suppose," Seth mumbled.

"So, if you are seeing real things –" Nadiya went on.

"Hang on." Seth stopped her. "You believe me?"

Nadiya nodded. "Why not? You believe what you're saying. That's good enough for me."

"Thanks," Seth said, with a grin.

"So, if you're right," Nadiya went on, "that means you're seeing something that happened on the moor long before the town was here."

Seth gazed across the moor. The wind was picking up, cold air pushed into his face and his eyes watered.

"Yep," he said.

"I read something about it in the school library. There's something that links the moor to what you saw at the Shay."

"What is it?" Seth stopped walking, turning to Nadiya.

"It's a story from a famous book called the *Anglo-Saxon Chronicles* that's like a record of everything that happened from around the 9th to the 12th century. It's the only record of life during those times. It's the only thing that was written down and survived. The *Chronicles* mention Yorkshire. And a hilly place like Halifax."

"Go on," Seth said, his chest tight with anticipation.

"The Vikings invaded this part of Yorkshire – roughly in the year 866," Nadiya said. "They attacked an Anglo-Saxon village at night in a place that sounds like here. They held flaming torches to light their way and chased the villagers down the hill and herded them into a big circle, rounding them up at a place called the Shaw. 'Shaw' means a wooded area – it's probably what the Shay used to be called. Then the Vikings slaughtered the

Anglo-Saxon villagers. Men, women and children – and all their livestock too. Every last one of them. They made the place into a terrible killing ground of blood and fire."

Seth said nothing. He stared at the moor in the dwindling light and saw the attack as if it was on fast forward. The village assaulted. The frenzied chase down the hill. The killing at the Shaw. The cries for help, the stench of death. The burning trees. He saw it like he was watching it though a pane of thick glass. It was soundless. It was shadows. But it was real. He knew it. Every moment of it was real.

Seth tried not to think about the face of the man. The Viking. He was too afraid to. But he knew that he'd have to confront that face again – one day soon.

17

Seth woke and stared at the luminous numbers on his clock. 02:03.

Next he heard a little whimper. Rosa. Her shining eyes found him in the dark.

There was a womble on the pillow next to him, wet with dog saliva.

"Thanks, Rosa." Seth smiled. He wondered if she wanted to go out in the garden. He'd let her. He was awake.

Seth walked barefoot through the house, choosing the floorboards that didn't creak, wondering why his dog was so restless these days. To the front door. Then into the garden, where Rosa lolloped onto the lawn and sniffed at everything and nothing.

Seth stared at the sky. The pinpricks of starlight. The vast expanse of moonless black. He took a deep breath in, then out. He felt OK. Safe in his garden.

Rosa looked happy too. She was ambling along the edge of the grass, like she was admiring the plants in the borders.

Then Seth's phone pinged.

A loud ping that echoed out across the garden and into the night.

Nadiya.

Wake up. There's a storm on the moor.

Like the ones that happen when you see

things. The trees are going crazy.

Seth stared up the road towards the moor. He was replying to Nadiya when it came.

Wind bursting down the road, tossing trees from side to side. The sound of horses' hooves heavy on the ground. A burst of light, flames held high. And the roaring of wind or fire. It was hard to pick the noises and visions apart. They blurred together like one great, invincible force.

Rosa scrambled up the steps and disappeared into the house.

Seth stood. He was scared too, like his dog. But he pushed the fear aside.

This was it. It was starting on the moor. Then down the hill to the Shay. The echo of the terror of

the year 866. It was frightening, but he had to see more.

He had to know.

Seth shut the door, leaving Rosa inside. She would be hiding under his bed now. His mum would be fast asleep. He wondered if he should leave a note to say where he was, just in case.

No.

No time.

Seth called Nadiya.

"Hi." Her voice was shaky.

"It came past here," Seth said. "It's heading towards the Shay. Noise and light. I can still hear it."

"Are you OK?"

"Yeah. You?"

"Fine."

"I'm going to have a look," Seth said.

Silence on the end of the line. Seth knew Nadiya was going to tell him not to. He was ready with a reason to go.

He had to know. He had to understand.

"Seth?" Nadiya said. "Wait for me. I'm coming too."

18

A taxi flashed past on the Huddersfield Road, but apart from that they were on their own. Two kids under the pale glow of the street lights while the rest of the town slept.

They walked along the main road, past the bus depot and the shop, until they were above the Shay. Over the fence and through the gaps between the trees, then they could see lights and hear noises

from the pitch, as if there was a match on. But they couldn't see anything in detail.

"We need to get closer," Seth said, wondering if he should really be involving Nadiya in this.

"Yes. Under the fence?" Nadiya said, pointing at a rough narrow path that could have been a fox or badger track.

Then they stared at each other in the almost dark. Face to face. They didn't need to speak. They understood each other.

"Come on," they said together.

19

Under the fence, careful to avoid a string of barbed wire, then they were scrambling down a dry earthy slope, rippling with tree roots. Next to the South Stand now. Then level with its corrugated iron roof. And the nearer they got to the pitch the more Seth could smell that musty meaty smell.

It felt like a warning. To stay away.

Seth ignored it.

It was hard to look at the pitch from up here.

They needed all their attention to make it safely down the hill, to not fall or tear their clothes – or skin. But Seth could hear terrible things.

Cries.

Shouts.

Roars.

They almost tumbled the last few metres, but an oak tree with its twisted roots exposed broke their fall.

"Lucky," Nadiya whispered, as they sheltered behind the oak tree from the chaos of roaring, shouting, screaming.

Seth said nothing. Just stared, open mouthed.

"Tell me," Nadiya said, looking too.

But Seth couldn't speak. He could only stare at the shadows before him. Shadows – that's what Nadiya had called them. The shapes from the past that he could see and she couldn't.

A circle of flaming torches, held high by men on horses.

And there, in the centre of the circle, a dozen, maybe twenty people, cowering. Men, women and children. Dogs too, snapping hopelessly at the men with weapons.

The smell of blood was overpowering. Seth retched as he stared, doubled over as if the pain in his stomach was too intense to bear. He felt Nadiya's hand on his shoulder. But he couldn't react. He could only watch.

Now some of the Vikings were slipping down from their horses, with spears and axes, approaching the huddled people. People without weapons. The Vikings chopping at them like you might at nettles blocking a path.

They attacked the men first. Men who stood defiant before their children and their women,

protecting them. But the Vikings cut them down. And when the men fell, they killed the women. Then the children. The thud of the axe blows. The screams of those being hacked into, torn apart. The grass all around them pooling black with blood. The wind howled like it was some terrible creature being tortured too. And Seth remembered what Nadiya had called it.

A killing ground.

Her description was perfect.

Finally, two cowering dogs, exhausted by trying to defend their masters, were slaughtered by a Viking with a heavy, curved axe. Their yelps of agony echoed around the stadium.

At last, silence. A silence heavy with death and horror.

Seth's eyes burned with what he'd seen, then he vomited, gagging and retching as sick and saliva

pulsed out of his mouth and onto the tree roots.

As he doubled over, one of the horsemen reared up on his mount and stared at Seth, his long hair flowing wild behind him. The man grinned, showing perfect strong teeth, then steered his horse towards Seth and Nadiya, slow deliberate steps as he peered into the trees where the pair were hiding.

Nadiya held onto Seth, to keep him from falling. But all she could see was the dark pitch and empty stands of a football stadium at night. And all she could hear was the howling of the wind.

Seth looked at her, his eyes flitting from her face to the slope behind them.

"We have to run," he said. "Now."

And they ran.

Out of the Shay.

Hard up the hill.

Past Seth's.

To Nadiya's.

Then, once Seth knew Nadiya was safe behind her front door, he walked home. His skin tingled, far too hot and cold at the same time. His whole body felt sensitive to every movement of air and light. He longed for the safety of his garden, his house, his bedroom, his bed. To forget the bloody massacre he'd just witnessed inside the Shay.

But Seth would not find safety tonight.

20

Seth had been in bed for half an hour, restless and awake, when he heard something.

He got up and walked past Rosa's sleeping body, then opened his skylight.

Right there in the garden. On the lawn.

The circle of flames.

Seth gasped. How long before it came into the house?

He took a deep breath and looked again.

The intensity of the flames had faded a little.
So now all he could see was the Viking, who was
staring up at Seth, grinning, laughing, calling out,
closer and closer to Seth's window. Ten metres. Five.
The ghastly face was floating high above the lawn.

Seth slammed the window shut. What else
could he do? And – as he did so – the Viking face
faded as if drained of its power.

But still Seth sensed a presence.

Behind him now.

In his bedroom.

He turned slowly, expecting to see the Viking.
But there was no Viking. Instead there was a woman
in a pale gown. Seth stared at her in terror.

"You're seeing things?" his mum asked.

"What?" Seth whispered with a shiver.

"You're seeing those things that other people
can't see?"

Seth swallowed.

"How did you know?" he whispered.

"Is it happening now?"

"Yes." Seth could hear his voice wobbling.

"Come downstairs with me," Mum said. "I have to tell you something. About what's happening to you. And about ..." Mum paused, her eyes red-rimmed.

"About what?"

"About your dad."

21

They sat in the kitchen. His mum had a cup of tea, the steam coiling misty threads in front of her face. Seth had a hot chocolate.

"He was an amazing man, your dad," Mum said.

Seth had no idea why his mum had chosen to talk about his dad tonight. But he wasn't going to stop her. This kind of conversation was rare. Seth had always felt like his dad was a mystery. But today his mum was opening up.

"He was a lot like you." Mum smiled.

Seth felt a surge of heat pushing up through his chest and arms.

"How?" he asked, wanting to hear more.

"Well," Mum said. "He was kind and helpful and loving. Thoughtful. And handsome."

Seth blushed and looked down at his hot chocolate.

"And he could see people from the past," Mum added.

Seth stared up at his mum. "What?"

"He called them shadows." Mum spoke carefully. "He saw them all the time. We'd visit castles and old houses and he'd tell me all the things he could see that no one else could see. It was really interesting."

Seth could feel his eyes widening.

"And you believed him?" he asked her.

Mum nodded.

"Do you remember when you were young?" she said. "You used to say you could see people walking down the road. Mill-workers."

"Yeah."

"And I told you it was because you knew about the history of the place. That, because you knew about how life used to be, then of course you could imagine it."

"That's not true, then?" Seth asked.

"No. I'm sorry. It's not."

Seth felt a rush of anger at the lies told to his younger self. But he hesitated, didn't let himself speak.

As the silence passed, Rosa stumbled into the room, her womble clamped between her teeth. She looked forlorn, as if she had been searching the house for them. She slumped on the floor by the kitchen door.

"So why did you lie?" Seth said at last.

Mum pressed the sides of her skull. Seth could tell she had a headache coming on. This was a big deal for him – and he needed answers – but he had to remember she was ill.

"I wanted you to see your dad as a hero," she said. "A superhero. You've always loved those comics of his. You used to pretend you were Robin, your dad Batman. So I wanted you to think of him like that. You were a child, happy. But I always knew you'd grow up. And you have grown up, Seth. Especially since I've been ill. So now you need to know."

"But what's so bad about seeing things from the past?" Seth asked.

"Sometimes your dad saw violent, frightening things," Mum went on. "Terrible things that troubled him, gave him nightmares."

"Oh. I get it," Seth said. "That's like me now. That's what I'm seeing."

His mum nodded. "That's what's worrying me."

More silence. Even Rosa, watching with her big brown eyes, made no sound.

"Your dad told me the shadows he saw started to frighten him when he became a teenager."

"Like me now."

A half-smile from his mum. "Yes."

"What do I do?" Seth said, a tremor in his voice.

Mum took a deep breath. "Your dad told me to tell you this if it started. He said it might be tough and frightening, but that you'd be OK as long as you always do what you think is right."

"That's all?" Seth laughed.

"Yes. That's all."

Seth frowned. So now what?

22

Seth helped his mum back up the stairs to bed, then he went to bed himself. Rosa followed, walking three laps of her blanket, before slumping down.

It was quiet outside. No noise, no lights, no madness. Now – in the dark – Seth could think.

He'd been told something frightening, something he didn't understand, but the fact that he was like his dad was important. The dad who'd died before he was born, the dad who'd left him a message.

Do what you think is right.

What did that mean? How did that help him now?

Seth could see the shadows of people who'd been here before. Mill-workers on the cobbled streets. Children in the corridors at school. Anglo-Saxon villagers tending their livestock.

Families being axed to death in a circle of flames.

And he saw these shadows just like his dad had.

But why?

Seth stared at the ceiling in the dark. All these questions. All this confusion. But he didn't feel helpless any more.

The knowledge that he was like his dad, that this was something that made him like his dad, made him feel stronger, like he could cope with whatever the future held. It was a bit like when he

used to imagine him and Dad as superheroes, but better.

Seth resolved not to run from what was happening.

He would run to it instead.

Then he'd be able to do the right thing.

Seth worked through everything he had seen in his mind. He went back to the beginning. To the Shay. It had all started that night at the Shay. The first time the floodlights came on in the second half, when there wasn't enough light in the sky. That was when the storm whipped into a frenzy. What then? What was the connection between him and what those people suffered night after night?

And why him?

Was it his fault?

Had he caused it? Is that what his mum meant?

Seth sat up.

No.

It wasn't that.

It was the floodlights. Not him.

The circle of lights on the top of the stands. Like the circle of lights created by the attackers before they slaughtered the innocent villagers. That was the connection.

The floodlights.

Seth knew it.

And now he was going to do something about it. Come what may, he was going to do the right thing.

23

Seth waited by the fountain for Nadiya. He needed to talk to someone who understood and it couldn't be his mum. She needed to focus her energy on getting well.

"Has your dad found out anything about Ernie?" Seth asked, as he walked with Nadiya between the two rows of trees up Saville Park to school.

"Yes," Nadiya said. "He's still in a coma."

They went on for a few paces, then Seth stopped walking and started talking. He went over the night before. He explained what had happened in his garden, what his mum had told him about his dad. He told Nadiya everything.

"So I think I know what the massacre you read about is," he said. "There was a circle of lights in the description, wasn't there?"

"Yeah." Nadiya said. "But why is it only now that this ... this thing is happening?"

Seth could feel his heart beating faster and faster. He was scared that he sounded like a madman. And maybe he was. Maybe he'd lost touch with reality. But he needed to see if Nadiya would understand.

"Since the new floodlights," Seth spluttered. "Since that circle of lights at the Shay, I've seen the circle of flames. The floodlights must be right in the

place where the massacre happened. The floodlights have brought back the past."

Nadiya nodded, speechless.

Seth went on. "So, we know now. We know the truth and we have to do something or it'll go on for ever. I can't bear for those families to be rounded up for slaughter night after night. I need to act. For them. We need to defend them! Do you see? We can defend them, Nadiya. We can be their defenders and stop the terror for them."

Nadiya stared into Seth's face.

"OK," she said. "How can I help?"

Seth grinned, his heart lifting. It was on. Together they'd stop the Shay becoming a killing ground night after night.

24

That evening Seth and Nadiya visited the new central library in Halifax. The town's archives were kept there in the cellar – which was built on top of an old burial ground. It had once been full of religious relics and the bodies of the dead, but was now a place where the town's memories were stored in documents and papers and old books.

"I did my work experience here," Nadiya said. "Do you remember? Where did you go?"

Seth grimaced.

"Oh no," Nadiya said. "I'm sorry. You were with the groundsman, weren't you? With Ernie?"

Seth nodded.

"Help yourself, Nadiya," Danny the archivist said. He wore a blue waistcoat and a pair of funky black glasses. "Just ask if you need anything."

Seth and Nadiya searched through endless papers, histories, documents.

"What exactly are we looking for?" Seth said, after Nadiya sighed for the third time and sank her head onto the pile of heavy books on the table.

"An answer," she said, her voice muffled.

"To what question?" Seth asked.

"That's the problem," Nadiya said. "I don't know."

So Seth and Nadiya went on looking at accounts of the past, at descriptions of life in

Halifax in days gone by. Seth could only hope that some detail, some story, would jump off the page.

An hour later it did.

"This is interesting," Nadiya said, looking up from the huge old book she was reading. "This book, it's about exorcisms. It's by a priest and he's talking about shadows. How past events can be so dramatic, so powerful, that they cast shadows over the present."

Seth listened without uttering a word as Nadiya described more about what the priest had written.

"That's exactly what happens to me," he said. "What does it say I should do?"

"Erm ..." Nadiya squinted at the page. "You have to face it. By showing it back to itself."

"How?" Seth said. "I don't understand."

"The priest gives an example," Nadiya went on.

"He tells the story of a room haunted by the ghost of a woman who had died there. No one could even set foot in the room it was that frightening. A force field of terror kept people out. But one man dared to go in and he made the ghost confront him. He pulled open the window shutters so the ghost could see her own reflection in the glass and it stopped. Just like that."

"But did he dare go into the room?"

"The priest says that the man had to believe it wasn't real. Only then could he take the ghost on."

"Not real?" Seth asked.

"Yes. It means that when you believe something awful from the past is happening, you have to stop believing it's real before you can defeat it."

Seth's eyes widened as he grasped the meaning of his friend's words.

"What?" Nadiya asked. "What?"

"That's it," Seth said, getting up from the table. "That's our answer."

25

Seth and Nadiya handed all the old books back to Danny the archivist, then went for a sandwich in a café at the Piece Hall. Seth looked round at huge square enclosed on all four sides by rows of arches and balconies and thought how beautiful it was. The only place like it in the world. If it had been in Rome or Paris it would have been crowded with tourists.

But Seth needed to focus. He knew what he had to do.

"So what next?" Nadiya asked, handing him a mug of hot chocolate.

"Go inside the circle," he said.

"*What?*" Nadiya raised her voice too high. It echoed off the far wall of the Piece Hall.

"It's the only way," Seth insisted. "Like you said, if I know it's not real I can defeat it."

Nadiya shook her head. "But they've got axes and spears. They're killers."

"They *had* axes and spears," Seth replied. "But they're dead. All there is now is light."

The two looked at each other. Seth stared at Nadiya without flinching, trying to look like he could do what he had just said to her. She stared back, then, after a long pause, nodded.

"So what will you do?" she asked.

"I have to face the shadow," Seth said, his plan taking shape as he spoke. "Find a way of reflecting

it back at itself so it stops. I need to be like that man in the haunted room."

"How?"

"A mirror," Seth said. "I'll hold it up to them and reflect them back to themselves."

"You're making it up now," Nadiya said. "How's that going to work?"

"There's a mirror in our spare room," Seth said. "I can use that."

"Really?" Nadiya said. "Sounds a rubbish idea to me."

Seth swallowed. He needed Nadiya with him on this. Without her he may as well just cower under his duvet.

"Come on, Nadiya," Seth said. "You've believed in me so far. You've not even laughed at me – much. I need you again. Remember when the Viking came into my garden? When I shut the window he just

disappeared. Well, maybe he saw his reflection in the glass. His own shadow? And that made him vanish – just like it said in the priest's book."

Nadiya stared up at the sky. Seth watched her and tried to read her mind. But, as much as he could see the past, hear and smell the dead of centuries gone by, he could never work out what Nadiya was going to say or do next.

All he knew was that, without her, he couldn't act. Only if she was with him could they defend the people who once lived on the moors around their town.

26

Seth took Rosa out for a long walk before it grew dark that evening. They went three times round the moor and he studied the shadows of the Anglo-Saxon village as they circled it. The energy of it was different tonight, charged and tense. Most of the villagers were sitting round a fire as one of them stood speaking, shaking his fist. Guards in chain mail stood on the outside of the cluster of huts. Each of them faced outwards, swords drawn, hands gripping

the silver handles of those swords. On their other arm, each one bore a shield. A silver shield boss glinted at the centre of each circle of painted wood.

Something was going on. Something had changed.

Rosa started to pull for home and Seth knew he had done enough – she'd sleep all night now. Just like his mum, who had already gone to bed.

Seth dropped Rosa back at the house, then headed for the Shay. He had the mirror with him. He'd arranged with Nadiya that he would find his way into the stadium through the fox hole, then watch and wait for things to happen, then message her to join him.

They both knew that if she was going to come out it'd have to be late and for as short a time as possible. Her parents would never let her be out on her own in the middle of the night.

It was dark and cool in the woods at the side of the Shay. Seth could hear the last buses arriving at the depot, the calls of drivers as they clocked off. The noises faded and he felt more and more alone. Alone and afraid. What was he thinking of? Taking on a violent haunting with – what? – a mirror.

Whatever. He needed to do this.

But first Seth had to wait. In silence. In darkness.

Until a breeze started up. Gentle at first. Seth could hear the tapping of wires on the metal of the stands. Leaves thrashing and swirling. The smell of burning on the wind.

He messaged Nadiya.

It's started ... It's going to happen.

The storm was whipping up quickly. Seth was

hearing things that weren't there. Smelling them, too. Meat, blood, the scorch of flames. Soon lights would be blazing. He swallowed down his feeling of fear. He'd have to control that. Nadiya would help him, give him the courage he needed.

Then a message lit up his phone and Seth cursed.

Dad caught me. I said I was going out to meet you. He's stopped me. I'm not coming. Don't do it. N x

Lights and screams were streaming down the hill now. The victims' cries were louder and stronger than the chaos of the storm.

And there stood Seth.

Alone.

Vulnerable.

Defenceless.

His head spinning with questions.

Did he really know what would happen if he carried out this crazy plan?

And, without Nadiya, who would ever know what had happened?

Seth's legs twitched with the urge to run. He wanted to leave this madness, like Nadiya had told him to. This was beyond him. He stood and turned his back on the Shay. He could leave now, but he'd have to turn around again. One day he'd have to face the killing ground.

And that day had come.

27

Seth took the mirror from under his jacket and walked out from the cover of the Skircoat Stand. He walked onto the track that surrounded the pitch.

No more hesitation.

No more doubt.

No more fear.

He was a defender. He was going to stop this awful history repeating itself night after night.

The stench of blood and death was overwhelming, but Seth knew he could do this. His new knowledge – that his dad had said for him always to do the right thing – made him feel strong. It gave him a purpose.

Once, over the advertising hoardings, Seth felt the soft grass of the Shay under his feet. He felt the heat from the flames too. He swallowed, then looked forward with a fixed gaze. The stands were full of shadows and flashes of light forming shapes now. Horses. People. Warriors.

Seth forced himself to look through the wind and the rain into the circle of flame, the middle of the maelstrom where villagers were about to be slaughtered. He moved to stand with them. Fire circled round and round. No sound. Just light and heat and a dark silence. The victims motionless. People from the village. Their children. Their dogs.

It would begin soon. Seth just had to remember it wasn't real, wasn't here, wasn't now.

And then it began.

The first thing he saw was an axe blade cut into a man's arm. Seth turned to look at the attacker. Then he heard screams and cries and felt his chest almost explode with that feeling of dread.

Times ten.

Times a hundred.

It was horrible. It made him want to vomit.

But Seth moved towards the attacker, the mirror held out in front of him. Shapes were emerging from the darkness. Then the flank of a horse hit Seth. He fell hard, dropping his mirror. He scrambled at the ground in horror.

It hadn't smashed.

But he had no time to feel good about that. Seth was a part of history now. He was the one to

defend the villagers, to end the massacre. He stood. He faced the line of giant warriors, all armed with blades of flashing metal.

Seth held the mirror up towards the circle of men around him. To their shouting, snarling, mocking faces. To their rage and bloodlust.

The smell of meat still hung there. The fierce men stood in their circle.

Seth's legs buckled. He retched.

What now? He was nothing but a boy with a mirror. He had no back up. No Plan B.

Why had he thought he could stop this? It was madness. He was mad. But he wouldn't be mad for long. He'd be dead.

28

Seth crouched in fear.

As he cowered, the mirror in front of him, he saw the attackers slip one by one from their horses, gripping their weapons as they moved towards the villagers, who were in their huddle behind Seth.

The Viking men were huge. And now they had the villagers and Seth at their mercy.

Seth felt his hands tremble and the urge to turn and run was overpowering. But he knew that if

he ran he'd have to face this shadowy horror again and again until he took action.

The attackers were moving closer now, hunters transfixing their prey in a circle.

What had he been thinking?

Seth would have laughed at himself if he hadn't been so scared.

Then one of the men eyed Seth and grinned, flashing perfect teeth. It was him. The man in his dream, from the flames, from the garden.

"*Sta og do*," the Viking said.

"What?" Seth whimpered.

But he knew very well what the Viking's words meant.

Sta og do meant *Stand and die.*

Seth stood.

If he was going to die, he'd die doing what he was here to do.

He remembered his dad's words – *always do what you think is right.*

Seth picked up his mirror again and held it out in front of him, pointing it forward. The Viking stepped back, pretending to be afraid, the warriors at either side of him laughing too. Deep, dark laughter that echoed round the Shay.

"*Hjelp meg,*" the Viking cried in mock alarm.

Help me.

The thud of axes was about to begin. The first woman was about to be slain. Then the dog would attack, its whimper as it was sliced in two. Next, the children. Two children, their skulls caved in.

No.

Seth had seen it before. But not again. Not if he could stop it.

Tears streamed down his face, then, using all his anger and grief to defeat his fear, telling himself

over and over that he was the villagers' defender,
Seth staggered towards the Viking and held the
mirror ahead, as steady as he could.

29

The giant Viking stepped back. He peered into the mirror, then swung his axe in a fast, arching circle above his head, ready to bring it down on Seth.

As the axe whistled through the darkness, the Viking evaporated into the light of the flames.

Just like that.

Seth felt a rush of adrenalin. Pure energy forced itself into his bones and muscles, the flesh of his body.

The attackers either side of him stopped laughing and stared. One lunged in rage, bellowing like a bull as Seth faced him too, the mirror shining ahead of him.

The second man vanished.

And now Seth knew he had them. They weren't men. They weren't real. They were shadows, nothing more.

Seth stood in front of each attacker in turn, the mirror facing them as they raised their axes to slaughter villager after villager.

But instead of carnage, the screams stopped. The attackers vanished into the night air and the villagers stood, realising they were safe and staring at Seth like he was a strange creature landed among them.

Then at once, all together, the villagers kneeled.

And one of them called out a word.

Aerendgast.

Seth knew what that meant too.

Angel.

They thought he was an angel.

30

Saturday morning, at the stone fountain. Nadiya rushed at Seth and hugged him.

"I'm so sorry," she said. Then, "You look terrible."

"Thanks." Seth laughed as Rosa jumped up, wanting to get in on the hug. The womble wedged between them, then fell to the floor.

"You have to pick it up and give it to her," Seth said, looking down.

"Eh?"

"The womble. You have to pick it up and she'll take it from you."

Nadiya nodded and Rosa took the toy gently and immediately calmed down.

"What happened?" Nadiya asked.

"It's OK. It's over. We did it."

"You did it."

"We did it, Nadiya," Seth insisted.

Seth told her how he had gone to the Shay. How the storm had picked up. How he had taken on the Viking raiders and – somehow, armed only with a mirror – had driven them away.

They walked up onto the moor, where the sky was a brilliant blue. The mist that had gathered in the valleys was burning off and Seth could feel the sun on his skin. The settlement of huts and people was still there. But it was calm now. The

families were back in their village, tending to their animals, working their plots of land. Seth felt like he recognised some of them from the massacre.

"You really think it's over?" Nadiya asked, linking arms with him.

"I do. But I'll be nervous at the next home match."

Nadiya smiled.

Seth hesitated, then asked, "Would your dad let you come?"

"Come where?"

"To the Shay," Seth said. "To the football."

Nadiya thought for a moment, then smiled. "Yeah," she said. "So long as it's not at three in the morning."

31

Back at the Shay five days later, Seth studied the pitch for traces of burning.

Nothing. It was as clear and green as if the events of the last few weeks hadn't happened.

Seth had been on edge about coming back to the stadium. But nothing catastrophic happened when the floodlights came on, and he knew everything was going to be OK.

The bleak atmosphere had gone too, as if a

dark mood had lifted. The South Stand were singing their hearts out and the team were playing well, pushing forward, attack after attack.

"This is great," Nadiya said, clapping hard and grinning.

Seth saw his mum smile at him.

He smiled back.

"It's a shame your dad couldn't come too," Seth's mum said to Nadiya, offering her the bag of Haribos.

"Oh, he's working. But maybe next time?"

Midway through the first half Nadiya's phone pinged.

Seth was watching an attack, tracking the ball as it squirmed out for a corner.

"Yes!" Nadiya said. "Ernie's coming out of his coma. My dad just texted. He's going to be OK."

Seth remembered Ernie's words from the day

this had started. *It's all going to plan*. That's what he'd said. And maybe it was true. So much had happened in the last two weeks.

He and Nadiya had defended the Shay – had put a stop to the deadly attacks of the past.

Ernie was on the mend.

Seth had learned something about his dad that made him feel that maybe he and his dad were – sort of – superheroes.

But what Seth didn't know was that, now they had stopped history repeating itself over and over in an endless, terrible pattern, they would be called to do the same again. And it would be sooner than he thought. It would be in London, when his mum was in hospital.

There Seth would learn if he had the courage to be a true defender.

Acknowledgements

I would like to say a big thank you to the children and teachers at Newcastle School for Boys, whose ideas have helped me so much with the Defenders books.

Thanks are due to Emma Hargrave, for her excellent and sensitive editorial guidance on *Killing Ground*. Thanks, too, to all at Barrington Stoke, who help me live the dream of being a published author!

Thanks to my wife and daughter who read my drafts and give me very direct feedback, and who support me in a million other ways.

Thanks to FC Halifax Town, Calderdale Council, Calderdale Libraries and archives, Crossley Heath School and to my neighbours for lending Seth their dog, Rosa. And to the real Seth White, for the use of his brilliant name.

ARE YOU A HISTORY BUFF OR A HISTORY BUFFOON?

Take this tricky QUIZ to find out how much YOU know about the Vikings and the Anglo-Saxons!

1. When the Vikings first attacked Britain, what did monks tell the Anglo-Saxons the reason for the attack was?

A. They had sinned and the Vikings were a direct punishment from the gods.

B. The Vikings liked to attack and kill for the fun of it.

C. It was so the Vikings could steal the Anglo-Saxons' wealth.

2. Vikings travelled in large boats across the North Sea, then upriver as far as they could. What would they do if the river became too shallow for their boat?

A. Build a canal or channel so they could keep going inland.

B. Carry their boat over the shallows, then put it back in the water.

C. Stop and carry out their attacks where they had access to waterways.

3. Kings were buried in elaborate graves, with weapons and their valuables. One of the most famous burial grounds in the UK is at Sutton Hoo. What was the king buried with?

A. A boat.

B. A chariot.

C. An early version of a helicopter.

4. In *Killing Ground* Nadiya talks about the *Anglo-Saxon Chronicles*, a history of the UK from 400 to 1066. How much of this book is true?

A. All of it.

B. None of it.

C. Most of it (probably).

5. Archaeologists have found the remains or ashes of animals like wolves and horses in the graves of Anglo-Saxon people. Why were animals buried with people?

A. So the animal's spirit could protect the grave.

B. To give the person the powers of that animal in the afterlife.

C. We don't really know.

6. Many Anglo-Saxons were kept as slaves by Vikings. But Anglo-Saxons kept slaves too. Why might you be a slave in Anglo-Saxon times?

A. You chose to become a slave because you were so poor.

B. You had been captured by another tribe and forced into slavery.

C. You had no mum or dad and people could enslave children who had no one to look after them.

7. 'Blood Eagle' was a Viking method of killing Anglo-Saxon leaders. What was it?

A. You were set free and an eagle was released to hunt you down and kill you.

B. Your ribs were torn open and your insides stretched out on the ground in front of all your people.

C. You were put on a tower at the height of an eagle's flight and bled to death.

8. When a Viking was killed in battle he would keep his sword in his hand even in death. Why?

A. Because with a sword in the hand Vikings believed they would go to Valhalla, their heaven. Without a sword, they wouldn't.

127

B. To trick people into thinking they were dead, then they could jump up and take part in the battle again.

C. Because the sword handles represented their mothers' hands, which meant they could die holding them.

9. **According to the *Anglo-Saxon Chronicles*, where was the first place the Vikings attacked in the UK?**

A. London, along the wide banks of the river Thames.

B. A small island off the north east coast.

C. York, the largest city in the north of England.

10. **Lots of people in the UK today originate from the Vikings, Anglo-Saxons and Celts (all from mainland Europe). But what percentage of people in the UK today are entirely from the islands of the UK?**

A. 40%

B. 4%

C. 0%

Answers on the next page ☞

ANSWERS

1: A
Monks told the Anglo-Saxons the Vikings had been sent by God to punish them. They did this to make them behave better and worship God more.

2: B
Vikings would carry their boats upstream until there was enough water to use them again.

3: A
The king was buried in a boat with lots of other possessions.

4: C
Most of it is thought to be true, but the people who wrote it missed out history they didn't like, or exaggerated other bits to make their masters look good. A bit like the media does today.

5: C
Lots of people have come up with ideas that sound like they could be true. But we just don't know for sure.

6: A
Most slaves chose to be slaves. Slaves had to do work in return for food and a safe place to live. It was that or starve!

7: B
The Vikings did this to humiliate the leaders and so that anyone else who might want to be a leader would be scared too.

8: A

Vikings believed they would only go to Valhalla if they died bravely, sword in hand. It was a good way of making sure they kept fighting and didn't run away.

9: B

A small island called Lindisfarne off Northumberland. There was a monastery there with lots of gold and other valuables the Vikings wanted to steal.

10: C

None of the people who live in the UK are 100% from these islands. We are all made up of a mix of peoples because, in fact, many thousands of years ago, nobody lived in what is now the UK.

BUFF OR BUFFOON?

If you scored 10/10

You're a top-class history buff. Seth and Nadiya will be glad to have you on their side as Defenders!

If you scored 5-9

You have more research to do before the Defenders will add you to their team!

If you scored 4 or under

Seth and Nadiya won't mind. They are history whizz-kids and will gladly give you a lesson!

About Tom Palmer

Tom Palmer lives in Halifax in Yorkshire with his wife, daughter and a cat called Katniss. Tom loves living in Halifax, so he wanted to write a book set in his town. But he used to think that books couldn't be set where he lived. Then he read *Wuthering Heights* by Emily Brontë, which takes place on the moors near Halifax. It inspired Tom to write about the places he knows well.

So, *Killing Ground* is set in Halifax. On Tom's street, in fact – and in the football stadium next door to his house, and in the library down the road.

In Halifax Library, Tom discovered lots of stories about his town. These stories showed Tom that the history we read about in books – and see on TV – happened in the places we all live. The Romans used to march along a road close to where Tom lives. That might have happened near where you live too. There's history on every street corner.

Tom visits schools up and down the country to talk about his books – on history, on football and on rugby. Find out more at www.tompalmer.co.uk.

What next for Seth and Nadiya?

Read the rest of the

DEFENDERS

trilogy and find out!

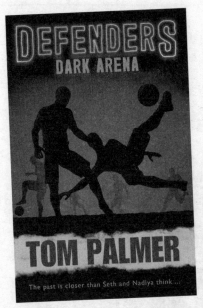

Coming August 2017

Seth and Nadiya's London holiday is fast becoming a nightmare. The city is full of ghosts from Roman times – and Seth can see and hear them all ...

Coming November 2017

At an Iron Age hill fort, Seth is haunted by visions of bloodied heads on spikes. Will no one help him lay the horrors of the past to rest?